Dear Parents,

Brendan Powell Smith does it again, this time combining his genius use of LEGO® building blocks with one of the most beloved stories ever told: the birth of Jesus Christ.

The main theme in this story is the role of the natural versus the supernatural. Natural is described as anything that people have control over and can explain. Supernatural includes those things that cannot be explained using human understanding.

The issues you may find most difficult to discuss with your child are Mary's pregnancy and King Herod's order to kill all children younger than two. Mary's pregnancy, known as the Virgin Birth, is a supernatural event that is unexplainable. Adults accept this event by faith. Many children don't yet understand how babies are made. So in some ways, children already accept childbirth by faith. To say to a child that Mary was special because she was chosen by God to be the mother of Jesus might be enough for now.

The more difficult issue is why Herod ordered the soldiers to kill all children under the age of two. In essence, Herod declared war on the children and there is no easy way to explain war. War is evil and bad because people die in war. You might simply explain that King Herod was afraid that people would worship Jesus as king instead of him.

In order to help explain some of the more difficult portions in this book, remember to give your child permission to ask questions, and listen long enough to allow your child the ability to answer his own question. Always be honest, as it is important to tell the truth when your child asks a question, but simple and brief answers are perfectly adequate. It is also important to read with your child and, based on your knowledge of your child, decide what you will focus on as you read together. This may help take the child's focus away from areas you don't feel comfortable discussing with them now.

I believe spending time reading the Bible with your child outweighs all of the uncomfortable feelings that will inevitably arise at one time or another. A great value of the Bible is that it challenges us to think about who we are and how we relate with each other. Remember: *The Christmas Story* has the power to bring us closer to each other and to God.

—Rev. Wanda Lundy, Director, Doctor of Ministry Program at New York Theological Seminary

First box set edition, 2015

LEGO® is a trademark of the LEGO Group of companies which does not sponsor, authorize or endorse this book.

Sky Pony Press books may be purchased in bulk at special discounts for sales promotion, corporate gifts, fund-raising, or educational purposes. Special editions can also be created to specifications. For details, contact the Special Sales Department, Sky Pony Press, 307 West 36th Street, 11th Floor, New York, NY 10018 or info@skyhorsepublishing.com.

Sky Pony® is a registered trademark of Skyhorse Publishing, Inc.®, a Delaware corporation.

Visit our website at www.skyponypress.com.

10 9 8 7 6 5 4

Manufactured in China, May 2016
This product conforms to CPSIA 2008

Library of Congress has cataloged the hardcover trade edition as follows:

Smith, Brendan Powell.
 The Christmas story : the brick Bible for kids / Brendan Powell Smith.
    p. cm.
 ISBN 978-1-62087-173-7 (alk. paper)
 1. Jesus Christ--Nativity--Juvenile literature. 2. Christmas--Juvenile literature. 3. LEGO toys--Juvenile literature. I. Title.
 BT315.3.S653 2012
 232.92--dc23
                                    2012017335
Cover design by Brian Peterson
Cover photo credit Brendan Powell Smith

Ebook ISBN: 978-1-62087-423-3

Editor: Julie Matysik
Designer: Brian Peterson
Production Manager: Abigail Gehring

The Christmas Story
THE BRICK BIBLE for Kids

Brendan Powell Smith

Sky Pony Press
New York

This is the story of how Jesus Christ was born.

In the town of Nazareth, a young woman named Mary was engaged to a man named Joseph, but they were not yet married.

One day God sent the angel Gabriel to tell Mary, "You will soon give birth to a boy named Jesus, and he will be called the Son of God."

Mary was very surprised and asked, "How can this be?
I am not even married." The angel replied, "Nothing is
impossible for God."

When Joseph found out Mary was pregnant, he decided to call off their engagement and send Mary away.

But an angel appeared to Joseph in a dream and said,
"The child inside Mary was put there by the Holy Spirit.
Do not be afraid to marry her."

Now at this time, emperor Caesar Augustus ordered everyone in the empire to register for taxes in the town where they were born.

Since Joseph's family was from Bethlehem, he and Mary set out from Nazareth and traveled for a week to reach Joseph's hometown.

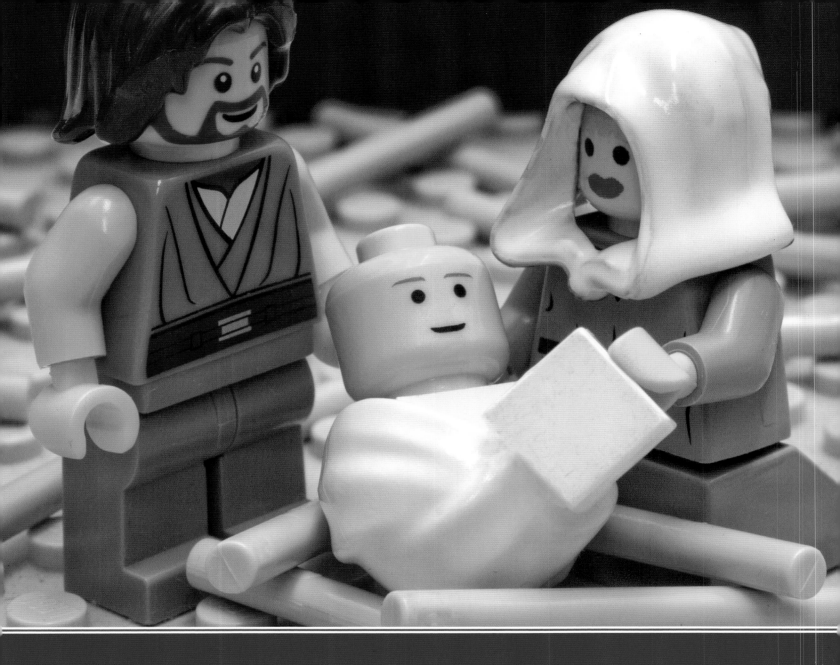

While they were in Bethlehem, the time came for the baby to be born. Mary wrapped the newborn child in swaddling clothes.

There was no room at the inn, so she laid the child
in a manger.

In a field nearby, shepherds were watching over their flocks at night when an angel appeared and said, "I have good and joyful news! Today a savior has been born, the messiah! You will find him wrapped in swaddling clothes, lying in a manger."

So the shepherds hurried away and found Mary and Joseph and the baby lying in the manger. The shepherds repeated what the angel had told them about the child.

At this time, some magi from the east arrived in Jerusalem and asked, "Where is the newborn King of the Jews? We saw his star in the sky and have come to worship him."

King Herod heard about this and he was very worried.
Everyone in the city of Jerusalem was very worried.

He summoned the magi and told them, "Go and find this child. Then return to me, so that I may also go and worship him."

The magi saw the star again, and they followed it until it stood still over the place where the child was.

Entering the house, the magi saw the child with his
mother, Mary. They knelt to worship him and presented
him with gifts of gold, frankincense, and myrrh.

In a dream, the magi were warned not to return to
King Herod. So they set out to return to their own country
by a different route.

Then an angel appeared to Joseph in a dream and warned him, "Flee to Egypt, for King Herod is searching for the child so he can kill him!"

So Joseph took the child and his mother and fled to Egypt.

When King Herod realized that he had been tricked by the magi, he was furious.

So he summoned his soldiers and gave them orders.

King Herod told the soldiers to kill all the children under the age of two in Bethlehem and the surrounding region.

Later, when King Herod had died, an angel appeared to Joseph in Egypt and said, "Take the child and his mother back to the land of Israel, for those who wanted to kill the child are dead."

So Joseph took the child and his mother and set out from
Egypt to return to Israel.

Joseph was warned in a dream not to go to Bethlehem, so they settled in Nazareth. There Jesus grew in strength and wisdom, and God's blessing was upon him.

Activity!

Can you find these ten brick pieces in the book?
On which page does each appear?
The answers are below.

A.

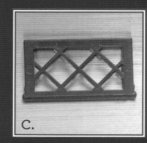

B.

C.

D.

E.

F.

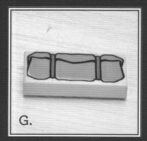

G.

H.

I.

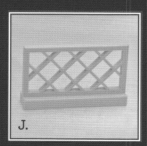

J.